UnitedHealthcare Children's Foundation®

ISBN: 978-0-9897937-0-4

Manufactured in the United States of America.
First Edition, September 2013.

Publisher: UHCCF/Adventure™
Author: Meg Cadts
Illustrator: Samantha Fitch
Contact: UnitedHealthcare Children's Foundation

9700 Health Care Lane
MN017-W400
Minnetonka, MN 55343

1-855-MY-UHCCF
www.uhccf.org

Oliver & Hope's

AMUSING ADVENTURE

Written By Meg Cadts
Illustrated By Samantha Fitch

"What should
we do today?"
asked Oliver.

Hope **SHrUgged** her wings,
which sometimes meant her back itched.

But, in this case,
it meant she didn't know what to do.

"I know!" Oliver shouted.

"We should go ride the
Super Scrambler rocket coaster
at Planetary Park.
It SPLASHES through an underwater tunnel,
CLiMbS up 1,000 feet in the air and then
DiveS DoWN the tracks at the speed of light."

"And that's just the first half," continued Oliver.

Hope flapped her wings very quickly. Now, sometimes that meant

Hope was scared, but in this case Oliver was pretty sure she was excited.

The two friends set off on their adventure, with Hope leading the way.

The path **zigged** and **zagged** and went up and down.
It reminded Oliver and Hope of the rides at Planetary Park.

... right up until

they got stopped by

a **crooked** little creek.

grr

Oliver growled.
Bears do that sometimes
when they're upset.

"Now what do we do?
If only we had a boat or a zip line.
Even a jet pack would work."

As Oliver explained what they didn't have,
Hope pointed out what they did.
Namely, the log that Oliver was resting on.

"You're a genius, Hope!
Since the log floats,
we can ride it across."

Oliver imagined he was splashing through the
Super Scrambler rocket coaster.

Hold on tight!" he said.
Oliver really just meant that for himself
since Hope, of course, could fly.

yaHoOoOO

Back on dry ground, but with
mostly soggy fur, Oliver said,

"Now we just follow the path
all the way to Planetary Park."

Hope saw that the path wound up
a **HUge** mountain and was
a little concerned.

"C'mon" said Oliver.
"We'll be there in no time."

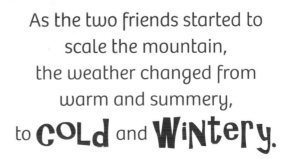

As the two friends started to
scale the mountain,
the weather changed from
warm and summery,
to **COLd** and **WiNtery.**

Near the very top, the climb got so **steep** that Oliver had an idea.

"Let's pretend we're on the
Super Scrambler Rocket Coaster
and we're **climbing** the tracks right before the big down hill."
Hope loved this game.

When they reached the summit,
they were startled by a voice
(since Hope doesn't talk, Oliver
was only used to hearing his own voice.)

"I'm Sherpa the Snow Leopard.
Since there's no way to go up,
I'm guessing you'd
like to go down?"

"Yes, but what's the best way?
The snow is awfully **Slippery**." Said Oliver.

"Well, before you slip, why not SLide?"
Sherpa said as she pulled out the biggest
leaf they had ever seen.

"Climb aboard,"
said Sherpa.
"Your ride is about to depart."

Oliver and Hope zoomed down the mountain
past the snow, so **fast** it felt like they were on the
Super Scrambler rocket coaster.
They had so much fun zipping through the
trees and swooshing into the valley below.

The giant leaf slid them all the way to the front gate of the park.
"Wait a second," said Oliver. "Why is the gate closed?

And **WHere** is everyone?

And **WHy** aren't the rides moving?"

Hope motioned to the sign that read "Closed For repairs."
The friends had traveled so far and had such an adventure
getting there, they didn't know what to think. Or do.

Oliver and Hope just stood there for a moment and looked at the rides, imagining how much fun they might have had.

But, after a few minutes, Oliver started to smile.

"You know what, Hope?" he asked. "These rides would have been fun, but I know where we can find even better ones –

TALLER ...

BIGGER ...

FASTER!"

Hope started to get excited. You could tell, of course,
by the way she was flapping her wings incredibly fast.
She knew exactly what Oliver meant.

"All aboard!" Oliver laughed.
"The ride to Sherpa Mountain
        departs in Five...Four...Three..."

And the two friends began their long journey back home.

UnitedHealthcare Children's Foundation®

Stories that inspire.

You can help us write the next chapter by helping those less fortunate.

This is a story of adventure and perseverance. A story of hope and imagination. And, in many ways, these same elements help guide the mission of UnitedHealthcare Children's Foundation (UHCCF), a 501(c)3 charitable organization. The UHCCF supports UnitedHealth Group's Mission of 'Helping People Live Healthier Lives' and also aligns under our enterprise values of Integrity, Compassion, Relationships, Innovation and Performance.

Each year, UHCCF offers grants to help children gain access to medical-related services which may be financially difficult to obtain. It is through these grants - and the shared commitment of our dedicated volunteers, donors, sponsors and recipients - that truly inspiring stories unfold.

The best part is you can be a part of these stories, which continue to write new chapters each year. If you know a family that could benefit from a UHCCF medical grant, you can help make an introduction. And, if you are able to offer your time or resources, we have many ways for you to get involved. Even the smallest tax-deductible contribution can help make a major impact in the lives of the families we work with.

Visit UHCCF.org for more Oliver & Hope stories and activities, and to learn more about how you can be part of our story.

UHCCF.org | 1 (855) 698-4223

UnitedHealthcare Children's Foundation
PO Box 41 | Minneapolis, MN 55440-0041